Other Schiffer Books on Related Subjects:

Olly's Treasure, 978-0-7643-3772-7, $16.99
Beyond the River, 978-0-7643-3741-3, $16.99
Baby Blue has the Blues, 978-0-7643-3732-1, $16.99

Library of Congress Control Number: 2011927212

Type set in Minion Pro

ISBN: 978-0-7643-3826-7
Printed in China

Published by Schiffer Publishing, Ltd.
4880 Lower Valley Road
Atglen, PA 19310
Phone: (610) 593-1777; Fax: (610) 593-2002
E-mail: Info@schifferbooks.com
Web: www.schifferbooks.com

For my two boys, Collin and Christian, who make every day an adventure. And for my husband Dave, who selflessly let me live a second childhood alongside our sons.

STOP
OPEN

Each week my brother, my mom, and I
take a trip to the grocery store.
We fill our cart with our favorite foods
like blueberries, bread, and a whole lot more.

We always stop at the deli,
where the butcher slices up our cheese.
And the baker gives us a cookie
so long as we say, “please.”

We make our way down the aisles
as mom crosses things off her list:
corn and carrots—but no candy,
I don't know how she can resist.

Sometimes my brother and I pick out a special treat
and sometimes we make way too much noise.
Mom always reminds us that we best behave,
‘though that’s sometimes hard for little boys.

So we try our best to keep mom pleased
as we go from aisle to aisle.
We also try to be polite
and greet those we know with a smile.

Seafood
fish
Shrimp
crab
cakes

For near the end of our trip,
at the lobster tank,
is our favorite spot to be.
Mom usually lets us visit a while
with these creatures from the sea.

The red lobsters in the tank
peer back at us with big and bulging eyes.
Their antennas, claws, and hard bodies
make them look like aliens in disguise.

Well, one day we got to the lobster tank,
my brother, mom, and I,
but this time, the lobsters all sat back
and then they started to cry.

"We are tired of being trapped," they said,
"Can you help to set us free?
We miss the dolphins and the whales
and all the creatures in the sea.

We miss the deep blue waters
and our comfy bed on the ocean floor.
We miss the starfish, the crabs, the oysters,
and all the sea life at the shore."

Mom shook her head and said,

“No, I am afraid we will have to let them be.”

“But Mom,” I said, “They need our help.

They need to get back to the sea.”

Mom marched on with the cart,
to look for the ice cream brand on sale.
So, quickly I snuck back to the tank,
and again, I heard those lobsters wail.

“Let us out, set us free,
and point us back toward the sea,”
they repeated again and again.
I wanted to help
and get them back where they belonged,
but you won’t believe what happened then.

One lobster jumped on top of another,
and then another one crawled on his back.
They kept jumping up on top of each other
until they made a very tall stack.

It was quite a sight to see, I am telling you,
those lobsters piled up tall like a tower.
I just had to help and I knew how,
I knew I had the power.

So I looked to see if anyone was watching,
and knowing nobody was in sight,
I took the top off the lobster tank
and then I squealed with delight.

There was a splish and a splash,
and a wave here and there,
as those lobsters crawled out of the tank.

Then they formed a line and started marching,
past the canned foods, the cashiers, and the bank.

People stopped, people stared, but mostly,
they all moved out of the way.
Those lobsters were on a mission—
Stopping only for directions to the bay.

25¢

Then they all shuffled in line to the exit.

The automatic door opened wide.

Those lobsters marched out

to the parking lot,

and then they hitched a ride.

You see, a tank truck was parked in the lot
and it was filled with water, icy and cold.
So they all scurried up and one by one
they plunged into the truck's big hold.

They said to the driver, "Head to the bay!
Take us now and please don't stop."
The driver's eyes grew so big
I thought that they might just pop.

So off he went in his big truck,
while the lobsters took a swim in the hold.
As the truck crossed a bridge,
the lobsters yelled, "STOP!"
And the driver did as he was told.

Those lobsters started marching again,
climbing out of the truck and down to the road.
They lined up on the bridge, standing claw to claw,
peering down at the bay as it flowed.

The lobsters' leader stood up on his tail
and raised one claw in the air.
Then those lobsters leapt into the bay
some even flipping with flair.

Once they landed they all sank down,
and only bubbles came up from the bay.
Then the bubbles moved out to sea,
they must have been swimming away.

I am still amazed by all that happened
that day we went to the grocery store.
But something far better
happened that weekend,
when we went on a trip to the shore.

My brother and I were building castles
and playing ball on the beach,
when our ball headed toward the water
and the waves took it out of our reach.

I dove through a wave or two,
paddling out to get my ball.
When all of a sudden,
there was a great big wave.
It was wide and awfully tall.

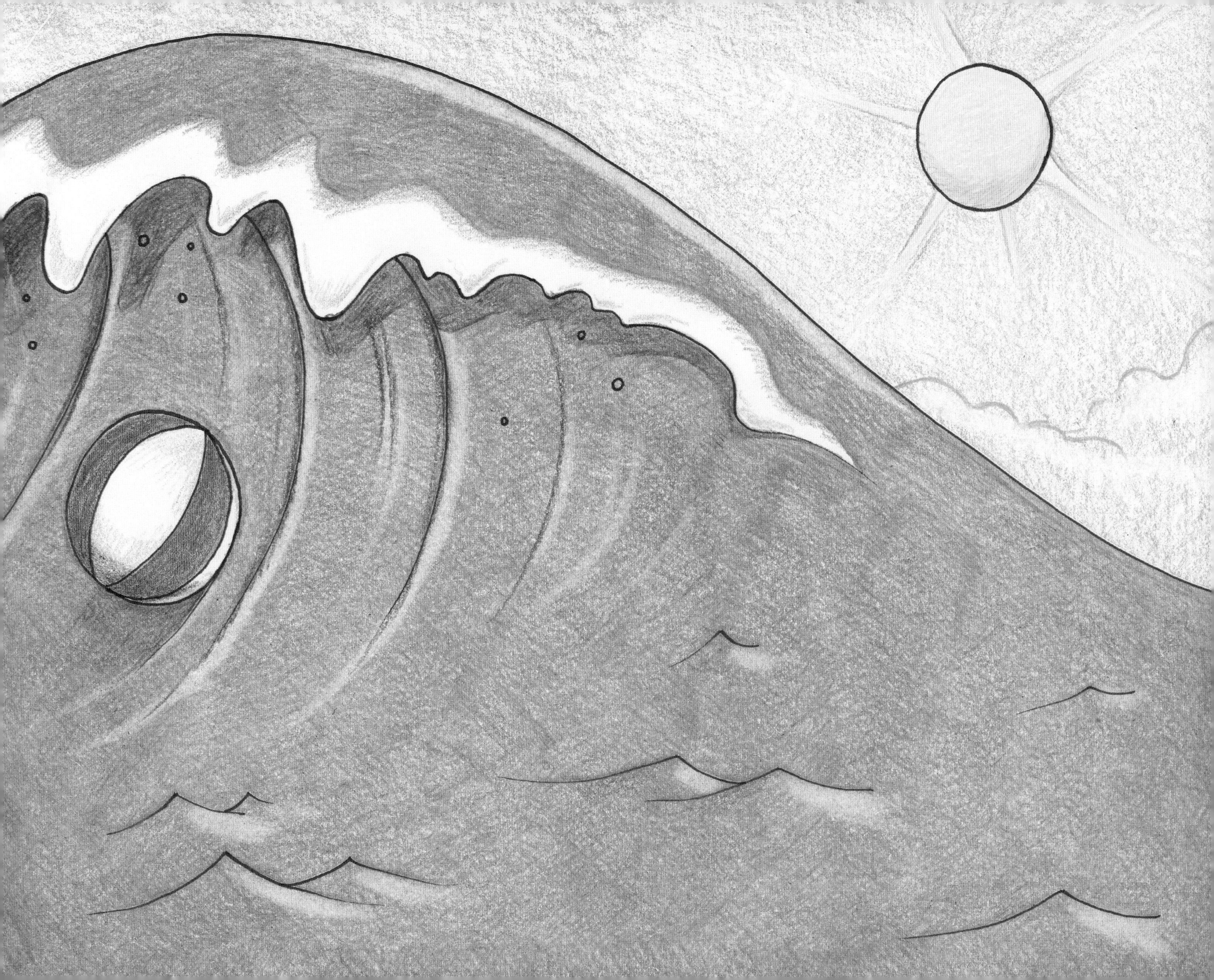

I closed my eyes, stuck my head under water,
and held on tight to my nose.
And as it passed me over,
I felt something funny tickle my toes.

As I came up for air and opened my eyes,
I saw the lobsters from the store.
And what started as a small clapping sound
grew into a very loud roar.

The lobsters were clapping their claws,
and the starfish circled me round.
The whales were singing a beautiful tune—
how I just loved the sound.

The oysters flashed their shiny pearls,
and a school of dolphins jumped over me.
All the ocean's creatures were celebrating
with the lobsters who were back in the sea.

The
End